Blood Ties

A CEDRIC O'TOOLE MYSTERY

10/21

Blood Ties

A CEDRIC O'TOOLE MYSTERY

BARBARA FRADKIN

ORCA BOOK PUBLISHERS

Library and Archives Canada Cataloguing in Publication

Title: Blood ties / Barbara Fradkin.
Names: Fradkin, Barbara Fraser, 1947– author.

Description: Series statement: A Cedric O'Toole mystery
Identifiers: Canadiana (print) 20190065117 |

Canadiana (ebook) 20190065133 | ISBN 9781459818255 (softcover) |
ISBN 9781459818262 (PDF) | ISBN 9781459818279 (EPUB)

Classification: LCC PS8561.R233 B56 2019 | DDC C813/.6—dc23

Library of Congress Control Number: 2019934023
Simultaneously published in Canada and the United States in 2019

Summary: In this work of crime fiction, country handyman Cedric O'Toole finds his life
turned upside down when a stranger shows up claiming to be his brother. (RL 3.4)

*Orca Book Publishers is committed to reducing the consumption
of nonrenewable resources in the making of our books. We make
every effort to use materials that support a sustainable future.*

Orca Book Publishers gratefully acknowledges the support for
its publishing programs provided by the following agencies: the Government
of Canada, the Canada Council for the Arts and the Province of British Columbia
through the BC Arts Council and the Book Publishing Tax Credit.

Cover image by iStock.com/davincidig
Cover design by Ella Collier

ORCA BOOK PUBLISHERS
orcabook.com

Printed and bound in Canada.

22   21   20   19   •   4   3   2   1

For my brother, Tom, and brothers everywhere

One

I SAW THE GUY coming half a mile away, the dust from his pickup blowing across my cornfield. Not many vehicles use the gravel road past my farm, so Chevy and I both stopped to watch. By the time the truck was halfway up my lane, the dog was off the front stoop and running toward it. Tail wagging, tongue lolling. Chevy never has been much of a guard dog.

The truck had Alberta plates, so the dude was a long way from home. He took his time climbing down, like he was stiff from hours of traveling. He limped toward me slowly.

"Cedric *Elvis* O'Toole?" he said.

I bristled. I've heard that little sneer often enough. My mother saddled me with that name, but she is long dead, and she couldn't help her love for Elvis. With his wraparound sunglasses and his leather cowboy hat pulled low over his eyes, the guy didn't give much away. But he wasn't smiling. About three feet from me he stopped.

"I think you might be my brother."

Now, I should say here that I have no brother. There'd only ever been my mother and me when I was growing up. We lived together out on this worthless scrub farm. She died when I was seventeen, and no one ever came to claim it from me. The only one of my mother's relatives who actually spoke to us was her aunt Penny. Getting pregnant at sixteen was an unforgivable sin in the O'Toole clan, Aunt Penny said.

So there could be a whole lot of cousins I know nothing about, but I'd have noticed if there was a brother underfoot.

I said that to the man standing in front of me. I couldn't see much of his face, but he was built like an oil drum. I'm a beanpole, even though I spend most of my days working on my farm and doing construction.

He grinned. "Half brother, I should have said. Steve Lilley's my name." He shoved out his hand. It was rough and callused, but his grip was friendly. He gestured to my front stoop.

"Can we sit down, Cedric?" He cocked his head at me. "Do people really call you that?"

"Only my great aunt when she's mad at me. Rick will do."

Steve limped over to my stoop and eased himself down. "You got something cold to drink inside?"

"Um…Coke?"

Steve made a face. "I guess that will do."

I went inside to get two Cokes. I don't drink the stuff often. It's so sweet it makes my teeth ache. But there were a couple of cans in the back of the fridge. I'm guessing they didn't have an expiry date. While I was opening them, Steve came into the kitchen and stood looking around. His eyebrows shot up.

I know the farmhouse is nothing fancy. It's about a hundred years old, and my mother couldn't afford to fix it up. She put in electric appliances and painted the pine cupboards and the old farm table bright yellow with blue flowers. But we pretty much left the rest of the place alone. I live here by myself, and so far it's suited me fine. I've been thinking I should fix it up a bit now that Jessica is coming over, but that's a story for another time. Now I could see it was pretty shabby.

I felt the tips of my ears grow red.

He peered over my shoulder into the fridge. I grow or raise most of what I eat myself. The fridge had a few vegetables, milk, eggs and goat cheese. "I don't have much right now," I mumbled.

"I passed a pub in town," he said. "We could grab dinner and a couple of beers there instead."

I thought of all the flapping ears that would be listening to our conversation. By morning the whole town would know about Cedric O'Toole's long-lost brother coming to town. My poor mother had had enough gossip in her time.

"I'll fix us something. And I've got beer in the cellar."

He seemed happy with that news and settled in to watch. I cut up some goat cheese, homemade bread, peppers and carrots, and put them all on a tray.

Back outside on the stoop, he downed half his beer before he said a word. He seemed to be having trouble getting started. "Your mother dead?" he said finally.

I nodded. "Long time ago."

"Mine died three months ago." He drank more beer. "Cancer. That was a bitch."

Words have never been my strong suit. But I know it must be hard to watch someone die bit by bit. "Sorry," I muttered when he'd been quiet too long.

"There was just me and her at the end. My dad died ten years ago. At least, I thought he was my dad. He was the only one I knew, and I always thought he was my real dad. But when my mom was dying, she told me he wasn't."

I finally saw where this was going. My heart raced as I waited. He drained his beer can and crushed it in one fist. "This is hard," he said. "I've been going over it in my mind this whole trip, how I was going to explain it to you."

"You want another beer?" I needed one. I was about to get the answer to the biggest question of my life, and I wasn't sure I was ready. Down in the cellar, I breathed in and out to settle my nerves.

"I brought us the case," I said when I went back outside. The sun was setting, and long shadows were creeping across the yard. Steve was scratching Chevy's ears. "We used to have a dog," he said. "God, I loved that dog. When I went into the service, my mother had her put down. Said she was old and sick, but I've always wondered." He paused and took a breath. "We grew up in Calgary. That's the only home I know. My mother said my real father worked in Fort McMurray during the oil boom. He'd come to Calgary for his holidays. He met my mother there, one thing led to another.

But when I was a baby, he went east to visit a buddy. Never came back. She never heard from him again."

He stopped again to scratch Chevy's ears and drink more beer. "Who's your father, Rick?"

I wasn't ready to tell him that story yet. I was already about to jump out of my skin. "Who's yours?" I shot back.

"They were never married. My mother called him Wild West, and she said there was a rumor he had an affair back here. Fathered a kid."

Wild West? In all the years I'd been wondering about my dad, the idea he was from out west had never come up. But why did that name sound familiar?

"Me?" I croaked.

"She thought I should know."

I was thinking, What kind of mother drops that sort of bombshell on her deathbed?

I thought mine was bad enough, carrying the secret of my father to her grave. But since I'm not great with words, only one word came to mind. "Why?"

"I was home on compassionate leave. I'd just finished three tours in Afghanistan. With this busted-up knee, I was on my way out of the army. I guess Mom thought finding my dad would give me something to do when she was gone."

"So that's why you're here? To find him?"

"Not especially. He left my mother with a two-year-old boy and a pile of grief." He looked at me, his eyes glinting in the sunset. Silvery blue, just like mine. "But it would be nice to know if I had a brother."

Two

I'VE NEVER BEEN much of a drinker. So after three beers I was nearly falling off the stoop. But Steve was just winding up. I stumbled to my feet.

"I've got some chores to do," I said before wobbling off toward the barn. Goats and chickens don't take care of themselves.

Steve limped along behind me. "Can you make a living off this farm?"

"I get by. I'm a simple guy."

We passed by the piles of junked cars and

gutted appliances scattered about. Thanks to Jessica, they were neater piles than they used to be, but rust and weeds were taking over.

"What's all this stuff?" Steve asked.

"I like to tinker."

He stopped dead. Looked at me with excitement. "Me too. I was a mechanic in the army, and I've been building engines since I was ten."

Halfway through the barn door, he spotted my old shotgun hanging in its case on the wall inside. It pulled him like a magnet. "Does this work?"

I shrugged. "I suppose. I hardly ever use it."

He peered at it. "Needs a bit of oil. I'll fix it up for you."

The goats had set up a racket, so I used that as an excuse to go inside without answering him. Inside, there was more junk. Old radios, toasters, lawn mowers—anything folks wanted to get rid of. I know I shouldn't take it all, but it's hard to say no. I have fourteen old lawn mowers, some of them buried so deep in raspberry canes that I can't even find them.

While I fed and milked the goats, Steve pawed through the junk. He was muttering like a kid in a candy store. "Some of this stuff is worth money, you know. Clean it up, replace a part or two, and you could sell it on Kijiji."

Kijiji. Jessica has been on me too to advertise my handyman business on the Internet. But computers and I don't get along. Like the kids I went to school with, they mock me when I don't understand. I'm a back-to-basics guy. I jury-rigged an antenna so I could watch TV, but I never bothered with the Internet. I have all the entertainment I need right here in my yard.

I finished the chores and headed back to the house. My head ached. I wanted to crawl into bed, but Steve was still going strong. He showed no signs of leaving. Back in the house, he opened up the fridge. Pulled out a pot and peered inside.

"That's soup," I said.

"That ought to do us for supper with a hunk of cheese and bread," he said.

"Shouldn't you be getting back?"

"Back where?"

"Well, to town. Or wherever you're staying."

Steve glanced up the stairs. "You got an extra bedroom up there?"

So Steve stayed the night. Not the quietest guy in the world. He woke me a few times, pacing and muttering. I was going to need earplugs if he stayed long.

The next morning I struggled awake at eight o'clock, surprised that Chevy hadn't woken me. Downstairs, Steve already had the eggs frying and toast ready. Chevy was sitting happily at his feet, catching scraps.

"Uncomfortable bed?" I asked.

He looked puzzled, then shrugged. "Just stuff. Nightmares. I hope I didn't yell."

"It's fine," I lied. "You can try sleeping downstairs if it helps."

"It's not the bed. It's a pretty good bed for a hundred years old." He poured me a coffee. "I've been thinking, this is kind of the first day of the rest of my life. I'd like to explore my options a bit. I could earn my keep around here. Maybe sell some of that stuff for you, help with chores, while I figure out what's next. I got nothing keeping me in Calgary."

That freaked me out. I've been on my own a long time. I like my own company, and all that stuff he wanted to sell was *my* stuff. "I don't know, Steve," was all I said.

Steve put a plate of eggs down on the table in front of me. "You ever heard of anyone called Wild West?"

I'd been replaying old conversations and meetings in my head most of the night. The name rang a distant bell, but I couldn't think why. "Don't know. Maybe," I said, picking up my cup. It took two hands, as if it weighed a hundred pounds.

"Who's your father then?"

"Don't know that either."

Steve sat and rested his elbows on the faded-blue-flowered table. "But you must have some idea. You've been living here your whole life. Relatives must have talked. In a small place like this, everyone talks."

"Not to me they don't."

He cocked his head and studied me. I could see the disbelief in his eyes, which had dark rings around the blue. Just like mine. My mother's eyes were brown.

"Don't you want to know?"

I thought about it. When my mother died, I'd gone searching for his identity. I'd always figured she'd tell me when I was old enough to handle whatever surprise she thought it would be. But when she smashed up her car and broke every bone in her body, I realized I'd have to find out on my own.

I wasn't in the best shape in those days, so I didn't get far by asking. I tried listening, hoping to catch a stray word. I tried watching blue-eyed men from the sidelines. Did any of them cry at the funeral? Did any of them visit her grave? Did any of them show a soft spot for me?

I went through a lot of theories. One possibility was my high school math teacher, whose dark-blue eyes still made the girls all fluttery. He was her teacher the year she got pregnant.

Another major contender was Todd, who ran the marina. He'd have been much older than her, but he had the money in the town, so he could pretty much get whatever he wanted.

I'd tried coming at the puzzle from another angle. I do that when I can't get an engine to work. What kind of girl had my mother been, and what kind of man would have interested her? I only had kid memories of her, mostly of her sitting on the porch smoking cigarettes and listening to Elvis. Or dancing with me all dreamy-like in the living room. Humming along. She'd loved Elvis. For years after her death his smoky eyes had looked down at me from posters all over the walls. There was still one in the bedroom where Steve had slept.

I figured any guy she liked would have had to look like Elvis. Jessica said women fell for him because he was dangerous and sexy, with killer eyes. Of the kids in my mother's high school class, the ones still in town after all these years had beer guts and buzz cuts. No one who looked like Elvis had stayed in Lake Madrid.

I shrugged a bit. It was too complicated to explain, especially with a hangover. "It seemed like a dead end," I said.

"But you must have theories."

"Like I said, dead ends."

"Jesus H., Rick. Someone knows! Or suspects. What about your mother's family?"

"We lost touch." Actually, we'd never been in touch. That was another sore point that I didn't want to share with a guy I barely knew. I knew where they lived, and when I was younger I used to drive over there, park down the road and watch the house. I knew my grandfather had been a carpenter. He still puttered around the house, but his back was all bent out of shape, so he couldn't work. I knew my grandmother had a bad temper. After I saw her kick their dog, I didn't want to meet her anymore.

Steve got up to clear the plates and wipe the crumbs from the table. The guy sure was neat. Must have been the military. "Well, this is a good excuse to get back in touch," he said. "Let's work our way through the possibilities. You have something to go on now. An Albertan who came here thirty-five years ago to visit a friend from the oil patch. Can't be too many of them."

My brain cells were beginning to come to life. "And what are we going to do if we find anyone? They'll probably deny everything. How are we going to prove it?"

"DNA."

"From all the guys it could be? They'll never agree."

"We won't know unless we ask. Who knows, maybe they'll be excited to find out they have two sons. Like I was thrilled to have a brother."

A thought suddenly clicked into place in my awakening brain. It was a question I should have asked right at the beginning.

"How do you know that? How did you find me?"

Steve tapped his temple. "The old noggin. After my mother died I was cleaning out her things. I found a letter postmarked Hawley Bay, February 1985. It was signed *Your WW*. He said something had come up and he couldn't leave till he sorted it out. I figured the something was you. So I paid a private-eye buddy of mine to do a little digging, and he came up with all the babies born in Hawley Bay in 1985. None fit the bill. But when he expanded his search to nearby towns, bingo." He pointed at me. "There was a little boy born in Lake Madrid in June 1985, father unknown."

"But...but..." My head reeled. I felt like I was in free fall. "That doesn't prove I'm your brother. Just because the letter was postmarked Hawley Bay doesn't mean your brother was born around here. You could have the wrong place, even the wrong year."

"But I don't think I do," he said, his silvery blue eyes staring into mine in a way that gave me the creeps. "But there's one way to find out. DNA testing ourselves."

The free falling got worse. "Oh no. There's only one doctor in town, and his nurse has lived here forever. The whole town will know before we're even out of the office."

Steve laughed. "On the Internet, you doofus! We order the kit on the Internet. You swab your cheek and mail it back to them, and they tell you how you're related. No one here has to know a damn thing."

He made me feel like an idiot. Like the world was galloping away from me, out into a future I didn't know or understand. Jessica makes me feel like that sometimes. I like keeping things simple, but it seemed like I was going to get dragged into the future no matter what.

Three

STEVE WASN'T TAKING no for an answer. So after breakfast we set off for the Lake Madrid library, which had Internet access. I kept my head down as Steve barreled toward a private corner at the back. I imagined everyone in Lake Madrid was staring at me. Rick O'Toole was at the *library*! He can hardly read a cereal box! My cheeks flushed just at the thought of their laughter.

Steve flipped open his laptop. He sure knew his way around the Internet. He found what we needed right away, but we were halfway through filling out the form when we hit our first stumbling block.

"What's your address?" he asked.

"Why?"

"So they can mail the kit."

I get maybe one or two dozen pieces of mail a year, mostly junk. I pictured Molly at the post office, staring at this strange box, addressed to me, with *DNA test kit* printed on it. Before nightfall half the town would know.

"We can't use my address."

"Why not?"

"Do you live in a small town?"

He studied me. "Okay. I'll sign up for a post-office box."

"People will still talk. A stranger comes to town and orders a DNA kit?"

"Well, Jesus H. It's got to go somewhere!"

"There's another post office in Hawley Bay. Only a twenty-minute drive away."

"So we have to go all the way to another town to get this damn PO box before we can do anything?"

I shrugged. "We've already waited thirty-four years."

Annoyed, Steve closed his laptop, shoved back his chair and headed out of the library, leaving me to scramble after him. Lots of curious eyes followed us.

The side trip to Hawley Bay took the rest of the morning, but we found a café there with Internet access and finished ordering the kits. I breathed easier now that we were out of Lake Madrid.

"This will take a few weeks," Steve said when we'd finished. "But we don't have to twiddle our thumbs. We can nose around town and see what people remember from the 1980s."

I winced. Steve's idea of nosing around would start the rumors flying. We might share the same blue eyes and love of tinkering, but he was a bulldozer compared to me. "Before you go stirring things up, let me ask a few people. Much easier than a stranger asking."

I could tell he was itching to get at it, but he seemed to get my point. I left him back at the farm, heading to the barn to "make myself useful." I piled a few eggs, goat's milk and organic lettuce into the truck and drove back toward Lake Madrid. My aunt Penny's grocery store has been at the crossroads outside town for as long as anyone can remember. Every year she grows a little more shriveled, like a parsnip forgotten in the cellar. But she knows every secret in town.

There's a fancy new grocery store on the highway outside Hawley Bay. It's taken away some of her business, but lots of village folk still come to Aunt Penny's for a bit of gossip and local produce. Even the cottagers are starting to buy my eggs and cheese, which she sells under the counter in the back. She's been after me to get a license. But that means paperwork. Not my strong suit.

As I helped her move some boxes and load up the shelves, I tried to figure out how to get her talking. She always snaps shut like a clam whenever I ask about my past.

I decided to stick as near to the truth as possible. Aunt Penny can spot my lies a mile off. "I got a friend visiting from Calgary," I started, with my head deep in the fridge. "He wants to trace his roots. He thinks his father came to these parts from Alberta. You know anyone who moved from Alberta... maybe thirty, forty years ago?"

Aunt Penny didn't answer, and I wondered if she was getting deaf. I knew her eyesight was going. But when I pulled my head out of the fridge, she was giving me the Aunt Penny look. The *What is going on, Ricky?* look.

I plowed on. "Apparently he worked in the oil sands."

"What friend?"

I shrugged. "Just a guy. Name's Steve."

She crossed her arms. "You don't have any friends from Calgary."

It pissed me off that she knew me so well. Knew that I didn't have many friends period. "Well, he was in the service. Traveled around."

"Where did you meet this Steve from Calgary?"

I turned to walk up the aisle to unload the next box, trying to buy myself time. I should have thought this through better. Whatever story I made up now was going to have to last me. "On a jobsite last year. He's just passing through."

She pursed her lips. "What makes him think his father is here?"

"A letter his father sent to his mother."

She gave me another long look, like she was weighing her answer. "Then why doesn't he ask his father?"

"Um…" I looked away. More lies to make up on the fly. "They lost touch. Listen, it's no big deal. He's just curious, and I figured if anyone knew, it would be you."

It was Aunt Penny's turn to look away. To get busy arranging broccoli. "Well, Ricky, I don't. I've been here eighty years, and I don't know anybody who came from out west or anyone who worked in the oil fields. Except—" Her mouth snapped shut.

I let that go. "What about in another town? Hawley Bay?"

She broke a stalk off angrily. "If they did, I never heard about it. Now there's a crate of milk out back, so jump to it before it curdles."

Afterward I turned the conversation over in my mind. I'd never been able to keep anything from her, and she knew I was hiding something. That would be enough to make her annoyed. But there was something else going on. She hadn't wanted to know about Steve. Aunt Penny is the only family I have. In her own way, she fusses over me like a mother cat. She's always worried about me living out on the farm by myself. She should be happy I have a new friend. But she didn't even ask to meet him.

It was like Aunt Penny was hiding something too.

Four

I WAS STILL puzzling over this as I drove away. Aunt Penny doesn't believe in coddling people, least of all me. She usually lets me have it with both barrels when she's mad at me. Something had spooked her. Something she'd decided I shouldn't know. Why? Years ago when she refused to talk about my father, I'd figured she was protecting my mother— or even my father, if he was a married guy in town. It hadn't occurred to me that maybe she was protecting me.

But I'm a grown man now, not a grief-stricken teenager. Does she still think I can't handle the truth? What's so terrible that I have to be protected from it? Someone else in the town must know. Someone who wouldn't care about protecting me.

Steve had given me some money for extra groceries, which I'd bought under Aunt Penny's disapproving stare. Now I had to pick up more beer. He went through more beer in a day than I did in a month. As I drove down the main street toward the beer store, I thought about who I could ask. I know almost everyone in the village, but I've never been good at small talk. So this was going to be awkward. Plus, my mother, like me, was a dreamer and a loner, and she didn't have many friends for me to talk to. I was going through the very short list when I spotted Nancy's Garage up ahead.

Nancy's Garage used to be Gus's Service

Station and Garage, sitting on a dusty lot at the edge of the village. But times change. When a fancy new Esso opened up on the main highway, Gus lost his gas customers and had to close the pumps down. He ran the repair shop until he developed cancer and couldn't even stand up. Nancy has always been a better mechanic than her husband. But he still sits in his wheelchair in the back office, bossing her around and trying to claim all the credit. They fight like a pair of old cats. Out of spite, Nancy renamed the place Nancy's Garage.

Nancy and I go back years. My truck is twenty years old. I can fix most of the things that go wrong with it, but she can do magic. When I rolled it into the creek a couple of years ago, everyone else said it was done for. Nancy found the parts to patch it together and get it back on the road. People laughed, but I had my truck back!

I rattled that truck into the yard and climbed down. I found Nancy in the service bay, underneath Jack Ripley's old Chevy. She scooted out, smudged with oil and rust, and tried not to groan as she stood up. Like Aunt Penny, Nancy's been around forever, and I don't know how old she is. Probably way past the age when you can start to collect a pension.

I started into my story about my friend from Calgary. Right away she waved toward the office.

"Let's go inside for a coffee, Rick. I could use one, and Gus could use the company. He's like a bear this morning, but if anyone can put a smile on the old bastard's face, it's you."

Gus looked even worse than I remembered. I could tell it wouldn't be long. His skin hung on him like a suit that was too big, and the yellow color had spread to his eyes. But a half-empty bottle of rye sat on the table beside him, and a cigarette glowed in the metal lid he used as an ashtray. Nancy shrugged, like she'd given up trying.

Gus spouted jokes about the weather, the crops and the terrible state of the bridge down near my place. Finally I got to my story. I told them I had a friend staying with me from Calgary, and he was trying to trace his father. Did they know anybody who'd come east from Calgary?

Gus was squinting at a stack of oilcans in the corner. "When?"

"Mid-eighties?"

"Well, your uncle Tommy was out west for a time. When was that, Nance?"

Nancy nodded. "Early eighties. When the oil boom was on."

That was news to me. I'd thought my mother's brother had worked construction around here all his life. "He didn't last long,"

Gus added. "But you should ask him about this fella. You never know."

Before I could think of an answer, Nancy jumped like she'd seen a ghost. "Wait a minute! Remember that fella froze to death up in the bush that winter? Wasn't he from Calgary?"

I felt a chill. It was a story I'd grown up with. Parents told it to scare kids off joyriding on the snowmobile trails. I'd always figured it was fake. "When was this?"

Gus was nodding. Still staring at the oilcans. "It was the year we built the new garage. Maybe..."

"Nineteen eighty-five," Nancy said. "There you go."

The chill crawled up my spine. That was the year of Steve's letter. The year I was born. "What happened?"

Nancy shrugged. "It was kept pretty hush-hush. Folks made up what they didn't know. All I remember was it was the dead of winter, and there'd been a huge snowstorm. They didn't find the body for near a week, not until the coyotes and crows got at it."

I tried to keep my voice calm. "What was his name?"

Nancy was on a roll, enjoying the tale. Gus still stared at the cans. "Police never said. Someone from Calgary, was all we heard."

"What was he doing here? Working?"

"Holiday," Nancy said. "He wasn't here long. I think he came for some ice fishing and snowmobiling. We never heard anything more, so we figured the body was shipped west to his family. You could ask at the funeral home."

Gus's wrinkles cleared. He looked up from his oilcans. "Wait. The police investigated. They should have a file at the station. That's the place for you to ask at."

Five

I WASN'T CRAZY about the idea. My tongue always ties in knots the second I walk into the police station. Sergeant Hurley is only a few weeks from retirement but he's built like a tank and can still stare down the toughest crook. I always feel like he can see right through me. Like he knows all my secrets. Knows I sell eggs and dairy products under the counter at Aunt Penny's, even though he never says a word. There was no way I could look him in the eye and ask him about the dead man who might be my father.

Constable Jessica Swan is the other reason my tongue ties in knots. I can't remember ever feeling before the pure joy I feel when she smiles. When she puts her arms around me. When she tilts her head to mine and says, "Rick, you're impossible."

We're taking it slow and, so far, privately. I stay away from the station, and she comes out to the farm to visit. She laughs at the idea of anything staying secret in Lake Madrid. But I don't want all the tongues wagging in the Lion's Head. I'm sure she'll get tired of me, or get posted away, and then I'll have to face all the loser looks in town. I get enough of those looks already.

So I didn't take Gus's suggestion. The police station could wait. Maybe someone else in town would have a better memory than Gus and Nancy. Instead I steered my truck back to the farm. Coming up the lane, I saw Steve squatting in the front yard beside his truck. His truck was jacked up, and one wheel lay on a tarp on the ground, surrounded by tools and parts and the dog. Chevy jumped up at the sight of me and raced down the lane, tail wagging.

"Brakes acting up," Steve said as I came over. The tools and materials were laid out on the tarp in neat rows. Right next to him was my shotgun, shiny and oiled. Steve shrugged like it was the most natural thing in the world. "It won't blow up in your face now. I hope you don't mind I borrowed some tools from your shed too."

I should have said thank you, but the words wouldn't come. I picked up the shotgun. He was in the army. It's probably just force of habit, I thought as I locked it back in its case. Then I came back to watch him. Changing the brakes is an easy job, but he worked even faster than I do and reached for the right tool without even looking. It was like watching myself.

"Been doing this since I built my first go-kart when I was ten," he said with a grin. "That's when I knew this was going to be my life." He nodded to one of the sheds in my back field. "I see you got a couple of go-karts of your own back there. We could go racing sometime."

I avoided his eyes. "I haven't tried them out in years."

He hefted the wheel back into place and tightened the lug nuts. After doing a test drive, he climbed down from the truck and wiped his hands. "Done. Time for a beer and a catch-up. You got a look on your face."

I wish everyone would stop reading my mind, I thought, going inside for the beer. I filled him in on the man who had frozen to death. "Did your father like winter sports? Ever drive a snowmobile?" I asked.

Steve was staring at the ground. He looked sad. "My mother didn't tell me much. No time. But I was always a bit of a daredevil, liked machines and speed and stuff. Sometimes she'd complain I was just like my father. She said he'd go snowmobiling and dirt biking in the foothills west of Calgary. I thought she meant my stepdad. But I never remembered him doing that, so maybe she meant my real father."

"What else did she say about him?"

He lifted his beer. "Well, she didn't like any alcohol in the house. My father—I mean, Harry—hardly drank, but when I was a teenager...hell, what eighteen-year-old doesn't get into the beer? And in the service, overseas, jeez, we spent half our time buzzed. When I came home it helped with the pain from this." He pointed to his leg. "But I'd catch my mother watching me. Not like she disapproved. More like she was worried.

So maybe booze was a problem. For our father, I mean." He nodded at my beer, which I had barely touched. "What about you? Is that why you don't drink?"

I shook my head. I don't drink because I don't like the taste or the feeling. Or how stupid people act when they get drunk. But I used to like speed. As a kid I raced that go-kart full speed down the gravel road and tore up the logging trails on my dirt bike. I still love to ride, but my joy of speed is gone. Ever since I identified what was left of my mother's body plastered against the rock face she'd run into.

Six

I WOKE AT dawn to the crack of a gunshot. Outside, Chevy was barking wildly. I rushed to the window in time to see Steve hunched over and racing past my vegetable patch. He was headed for the woods, hopping and limping as fast as he could move. In his hands was a rifle.

Early-morning mist still hung in the air. I ran outside in a panic. What the hell had he seen? I called out, but he'd disappeared. Chevy came back, her ears flattened with fear.

I went to the barn for my shotgun. I hate the thing, but it has its uses for scaring off animals.

The shotgun was gone, the ammunition scattered across the floor.

Calling to Chevy, I headed toward the woods. The morning was dead calm, but angry crows flapped and cawed overhead. I found Steve sitting at the base of a tree, hugging my gun. He was shaking.

"Steve, what the hell?"

He looked at me like he didn't see me. Blinked.

I could tell he wasn't there. He was somewhere else. I reached out and took the gun. That seemed to bring him back, because he rubbed his face and shook his head.

"Sorry," he said. "Crows. They...they were getting at the vegetables."

We said nothing as we walked back to the house. He was still shaking. When we got inside, he took a long look at the beer in the fridge. But he started in on breakfast. He flipped between fridge and stove without saying a word.

"Does that happen often?" I asked.

He shrugged. "Weird things set it off. This time it was the birds."

"Did the army give you help?" I was one to talk. Social services had offered me help more times than I could count. I'd sat in front of the counselor, quiet as a mouse.

"The best thing is keeping busy. Today I'm going back to Hawley Bay for an oil-filter housing for the truck. The poor girl took quite a beating driving across Canada from Calgary."

Once he'd gone I took the shotgun back to the barn. I thought about hiding it. In the end, I hid the ammunition in my bedroom. I didn't know how to help him, but at least I could keep us safe.

Breathing easier, I tackled a few chores around the place. My first surprise was the garden shed. The potting table was tidy, and the floor was swept. All the tools were hung on nails along the wall. Military neat. This must be part of his keeping busy. It had its uses. I should tell him about the fourteen lawn mowers buried in the raspberry patch, I thought.

I pulled up some carrots and onions to take to Aunt Penny's place. Beside her cash register was a stack of newspapers, including the local *Madrid News*. As Aunt Penny paid me, she said nothing about Steve, but the newspapers gave me an idea.

So for the second time in two days, I walked into the library. This time I didn't feel like an idiot. I was too excited to pay any attention to the curious looks.

The library had a small stack of *Madrid News*. I looked through them, but none were older than six months. A sign told me to ask the librarian for older editions. I groaned. Susie Wilson had been a bookworm even back in school. I'd never dared talk to her. I kept my eyes down as I mumbled my question.

She brightened. "How old?"

"Nineteen eighty-five?"

Her smile disappeared. "We don't keep newspapers that old. We don't have the storage space."

I bobbed my head. The little library was barely the size of a living room. "Does anybody keep them?"

"Oh yes, there'd be digital records in the main branch down in Queenston. Mind you, that far back the papers might be on microfilm."

I opened my mouth to ask what microfilm was, but stopped. No point looking like even more of an idiot. My heart sank. I didn't want to drive two hours, maybe for nothing. "You're sure they have the *Madrid News*?"

"Well, we can check." Susie turned to her computer and typed and clicked her way through a blur of screens. Finally she frowned at the screen. "Yes, they do, but you have to request them in advance." She laughed. "They're probably in some librarian's basement."

I sneaked a glance at her. "How do I...?"

"You want me to request them for you?"

"It...it's probably not worth it."

"You could always ask the editor. Dan Picard. He's been around awhile. I know he took a bunch of old boxes from the newspaper office when he became the only full-time reporter. Knowing Dan, they're probably still in his basement." She picked up her cell phone. "I can call him if you like."

I was already backing away. "That's okay. I know where he lives. Thanks."

Dan Picard had bought an old scrub farm that was even more useless than mine. Instead of trying to grow things, he'd let it go wild, and in his spare time he made furniture and carvings from the deadwood on his land. Chairs, benches and arbors were for sale in his front yard, in case anyone happened to drive by.

When I pulled up, three dogs raced around the side of the house, barking. I was just saying hello to them when Dan appeared from the back. A pair of safety goggles was propped on his bald head, and sawdust covered every inch of him.

"Rick!" He shoved out one dusty hand. Dan and I had worked on a couple of cottage jobs together. I'd built the decks, and he'd furnished them. We both loved creating things out of wood. But Dan also created poems, something that left me in the dust.

He brushed himself off and headed inside

to get two beers. I went around back to his workshop to check out his latest project. The burnt smell of freshly milled wood hung in the air. Two large planks of pine sat on the table, and others were propped against it, waiting to be sanded.

"It's going to be a dining table for the Harrisons," he said behind me. "A commission. I might even make a few dollars this year, to supplement the meager editor's pay."

I stalled, looking for a way to begin. I sipped my beer and admired the wooden bowls that lined the shelves. I ran my finger over the sanded plank. Finally he said, "Okay, Rick. My humble abode is nowhere near yours, or anyone else's, for that matter. What brings you here?"

I translated that into plain words. Grinned, suddenly shy. "Susie Wilson says you have old copies of the *Madrid News* stored here."

"That I do, in the cellar. I haven't looked at them in years. What are you looking for?"

"Nineteen eighty-five?"

Dan's eyebrows shot up. "Were you even born?"

I shrugged. "I'm looking for news about a man's death."

"Who?"

"I don't know his name. A stranger from Alberta. He froze to death out on the snowmobile trail. I figure it should be in the news."

"Why the interest?"

I guess old reporters never lose their nose for news. I tried to sound casual. "I'm helping a friend trace his family. A...a distant friend."

"I wasn't at the paper in 1985, but my predecessor did leave boxes of back issues. When I moved the newspaper office out here, I brought everything with me. You're welcome to check. They're a bit of a mess, I'm afraid. It will take a while to go through them. No guarantees."

"How many boxes?"

"Oh, could be fifty?"

He must have seen my dismay. He knew reading was not my strong suit, because a half beat later he said, "Do you want me to check them out for you?"

I turned red with relief. As I turned to go, I thanked him. He gave me another curious look. "You're going to a lot of trouble for a distant friend."

Seven

I SPOTTED TROUBLE the minute I turned into my lane. Jessica Swan was climbing out of her car, next to Steve and his truck. At least she was driving her own car instead of a cruiser, and wearing shorts and a tank top instead of her uniform. But Jessica thought like a cop. She'd probably demand to know what he was doing there.

I hit the gas and shot up the lane, dust flying. Jessica turned in surprise, and a smile broke her cop-like frown. She looked pretty then, her ponytail the color of a corn tassel and her eyes like the sky. Her uniform bulked her up, but without it she was as tiny and lean as a colt. She had to stand on tiptoe to kiss me. I blushed, still awkward with that.

But Steve was grinning from ear to ear as he reached out his hand. "Hi, I'm Steve, Rick's—"

"Steve's a friend from out west. He's staying for a couple of days while we fix his truck," I babbled.

Steve shot me a puzzled look that I pretended not to see. I slipped my hand into Jessica's. "Chevy could use a walk, so why don't we take her and let Steve finish up with his truck."

Chevy was snoozing in the shade of the truck, but she cocked a lazy ear at the sound of her name and the word *walk*. Steve seemed to catch on, because he offered to get some lunch and drinks for our return.

The back field was high with daisies and clover, but Chevy and I had worn a path through it to the woods. Bees buzzed in the tiny pink flowers, and I breathed in the sweet clover smell. I tried to figure out how to explain. Once we had entered the woods and were out of sight, Jessica pulled her hand away.

"Rick, you're jumpy as a cat. Who is this Steve?"

"He came out here to track down his real father." I told her about the mother's deathbed confession. "We've been asking around. Gus and Nancy said there was a guy who died in a snowmobile accident about the right time. They didn't know his name but think he was from Calgary. Do you think...?" I sneaked a quick peek at her. "Could you check if there's a police file?"

"When was this?"

"Winter of 1985."

"That's a long time ago. Those old files won't be on the computer."

"But they'd be somewhere, right?" I held my breath. Didn't dare look at her. I'd never asked her for personal favors before.

Jessica was quiet. She frowned at the ground as she picked her way over roots and rocks. "Steve is good with his hands," she said after a while.

"He was a mechanic in the army."

"He has unusual blue eyes."

I didn't say anything.

"Who is he, Rick?"

I didn't want to lie to her. We were just starting to get close, and lies wouldn't help that. But I never talked about my past, with her or anyone else. When I was growing up, kids called me mean names, and their parents weren't much better. Even my mother's family—aside from Penny—wouldn't talk to us. It was bad enough I had no father to show me how to hunt and fish and split wood like the other kids did, but my mother's shame became my shame. I wore it like a shield.

I felt naked without it.

Jessica's hand slipped back into mine. "Is he your cousin?"

I shook my head. The words stuck in my throat. I coughed. "He thinks he's my half brother."

Her hand tightened. "Then his father would be your father? You're looking into your father's death?"

I nodded. "I don't want everyone to know. I don't even know if I want to know. No one's ever wanted to talk about it. I figured it was probably some guy in the village, married with a bunch of kids of his own. A guy who couldn't admit to getting a sixteen-year-old girl pregnant. A guy who didn't dare look me in the eye."

"Out here in the country..." She spoke

slowly, like she was picking her way. "Lots of bad things are hushed up. You'd be surprised the secrets I learn. Teachers, priests, trusted friends of the family…"

The words shot through me like a hot poker. I've lived a pretty quiet life out on my farm, but that doesn't mean I don't hear things. I'd always thought my mother had had her one true love. The idea that she'd been forced had never entered my mind. That even in love, she'd been a victim. Yet it could explain everything. The silence, the shame, the fits of rage and despair.

Did I want to know? Did I want to know it was an act of violence, not love, that had created me?

Jessica stopped and stared up into my eyes. She seemed to be searching for words. "Are you worried? What you might find? Is that it?"

"No," I said, grabbing at lies. "My mother

died in a terrible accident. I...I don't want to learn that my father did too. I don't want to know that all our hard times could have been different."

Eight

I WAS PACKING up my tools to go to a jobsite when Jessica phoned the next morning. Steve had been up since three in the morning, reorganizing my third shed, so I had to run to catch the phone before he did.

"Are you free this morning?" she said.

"I'm on my way to the Oland cottage," I began. But something in her voice stopped me. "Do you want to come out?"

"No, I think it might be better if I meet you in town."

I gripped the phone. "Do you have something?"

"Yes. But I want to tell you privately, so you can decide what to tell Steve."

My heart lurched. I wanted to yell *what?* but forced myself to wait.

"Can you meet me at Tims?"

The Tim Hortons on the highway is the most popular place in town, with a lineup out the door in the mornings. "There are too many big ears there in the morning," I said. "There's a new café in Hawley Bay. Mostly the city cottage crowd."

I pushed my old truck as fast as I could to get to it in half an hour. Jessica was already there, sitting in a back corner against the wall. She had a notebook on the table beside her coffee and Danish. My heart was pounding, but I took time to order a coffee and croissant. Now that the moment was here, I was afraid to know.

Jessica must have seen my face, because she smiled and squeezed my hand. She spoke without opening her notebook. "I found a file in the basement cabinet. The accident took place in February 1985, on the snowmobile trail about three miles north of town. There was a police investigation at the time, but—" She stopped and shook her head. "The coroner's report and postmortem results are on file. The victim sustained a severe blow to the head that probably knocked him out, but he died of hypothermia. He was an otherwise healthy white male, height five feet eight inches, weight 154 pounds, age midtwenties. Fair hair and complexion, blue eyes. There was a tattoo of a heart pierced by a rose on his upper left arm but no other distinguishing marks."

Her voice was flat, like a cop in court, but now she stopped and softened. "Tattoos weren't as common back then. Sounds like he might have been in love."

I barely heard her. My mind was already racing ahead. So far, it all checked out. Blue eyes and fair hair like Steve and me. I was taller and skinnier than the guy, but my mother had been tall. This man was built like Steve.

"What did the police investigation say?" I croaked.

She flushed and played with her notebook. "Not much. There were no forensics or witness statements. He was drunk. The officer concluded that he missed a curve, went down a ravine and hit his head on a tree on the way down. His body, and the snowmobile, were found buried in snow at the bottom of the slope, about thirty feet off the trail. With the snow that came that night, you wouldn't have seen anything driving by unless you were looking."

I pictured the man's last moments. Would he have been too drunk to know he was dying? Would he have tried to shout for help?

"Was he by himself?"

She nodded. "The police assumed so, since no one reported the accident. He wasn't found till almost a week later, when someone phoned in a tip."

"Who?"

She fiddled with her notebook again. "The report doesn't say."

"No one reported him missing?"

"Nope."

"Where was he before? Was anyone drinking with him that night?"

"The report doesn't say that either."

I stared at her, but she just shrugged. I steeled myself. Now was the moment of truth. "Who was he?"

She lowered her eyes. "Look, Rick, I've already told you more than I should. This is a confidential police report, details withheld at the request of the family."

"Who's the family?"

"It's not in the file."

"That's ridiculous! They must have released the body to someone."

"I suppose." She reached across the table to take my hands in hers. "That's all I can say. If Sergeant Hurley ever found out I'd told you anything, it could be my job!"

I pulled my hands from hers. To be so close, and yet nowhere!

She looked hurt. "I've given you a place to start. If you can keep my name out of it, you can try asking Sergeant Hurley about the investigation. After more than thirty years, the confidentiality probably doesn't matter all that much."

"But if Hurley only knows what's in that useless report..."

"He'd know more. He'd know it all. He was the investigating officer."

Nine

SERGEANT HURLEY AND I have a strange relation-
ship. He's the one who first took me into care
after my mother went a whole week without
getting off the couch. I was four, and someone
spotted me trying to milk the cow and eating
carrots straight out of the ground. Hurley
was a rookie back then, and he helped my
mother out with groceries and stuff. He said
he was her friend. She didn't even get off the
couch when he took me away. Even thanked
him. I remember looking out the window of

the cruiser, eating the ice-cream cone he'd bought me and it dripping on the seat. I was scared he'd be mad, but he just ruffled my hair. Said it happened all the time.

A few years later he was posted away. The next time I saw him he was standing at the farmhouse door, hat in hand. Looking like a ghost. He tried to hug me, but I was seventeen by then. Foster homes had taught me a lot. All the bad memories came back, and I shoved him away. I barely saw the tears in his eyes or heard the words he said. *I'm so sorry, son, there's been a terrible accident.*

He called me *son* that day. He said if I ever needed anything, he was just a phone call away.

There was a time when I wished he *was* my father. Thought maybe he was. I'm not much good at reading people. My mother and I lived alone. She was estranged from her family and had few if any real friends.

So I didn't know if they had anything going. As a kid, I thought he was just there. Once I had Jessica, I found myself wondering about the smiles they shared when they thought I wasn't looking. But Sergeant Hurley has eyes like chestnuts and a body like a grizzly bear. He could have played linebacker for the CFL. Beside him, even Steve looks like a dwarf.

Hurley is back as detachment commander now, and he is getting gray and grumpy. He drives around town like he owns the place. He calls everyone by their first name, and he knows everyone's business, including mine. And that is the problem. He checks up on me, watches me when he thinks I'm not looking.

I knew he'd be way too nosy if I asked him about the dead dude. I wanted to keep this story private. I wanted to control the tongue wagging and the knowing looks. I didn't want to drag up old gossip my mother could never outrun. I didn't want him peering over my shoulder each step of the way. So I didn't take Jessica's advice. Instead, I decided to try my chances with Aunt Penny again.

Aunt Penny's shop was hopping. There was a lineup at the cash register, and every customer had a long story to tell. Aunt Penny looked like she'd been on her feet all morning. She leaned on the counter every chance she got. She hates any offer of help, saying she isn't in her grave yet. But I restocked the heavy water jugs and a few other things while I waited.

I'd moved on to charcoal bags by the time the last customer left. Aunt Penny even thanked me as she sank into her chair. But the smile didn't last.

"You're a ray of sunshine today, Ricky. What's on your mind?"

"My friend from Calgary—"

"Is he still here?"

"We've learned some things about his father. I want to ask—"

"I told you all I know."

I pushed on. "We think he died in a snowmobile accident just north of town before I was born. Do you remember it?"

She took off one shoe and rubbed her foot, saying nothing.

"That would have been pretty big news back then."

"I don't make a habit of engaging in gossip." She raised her head. "And neither should you. It's in the past. Best left in the past. That poor man paid the price."

"Then you knew him?"

"Ricky! Stop putting words in my mouth. I knew nothing about it."

At that moment the bell over the door rang, and Nancy burst into the shop. Her eyes lit up at the sight of me.

"Rick!" she cried. "Gus and I remembered

more about that man from Calgary!"

Aunt Penny was shaking her head, but Nancy didn't seem to notice. "He was a friend of your mother's brother," she said. "They met out west, and he came to visit."

Aunt Penny knocked a bottle of Coke off the counter with a bang. "Cedric!" she snapped as it rolled across the slanted floor toward me.

Nancy barely missed a beat as she scooped it up. "Gus remembered his name was Wes. Don't know his last name, but Penny, you'd sure remember him. Him and Tommy tore up the town a few times."

"Ancient gossip!" Aunt Penny snapped, going the color of a pomegranate. "I won't be repeating any of it. What can I get you, Nancy?"

Nancy rolled her eyes at me. "Right. If we could look into your aunt Penny's head, the secrets we'd find! But she has a point.

The man's dead now. No help to your friend to know his father was a wild one. I'm wondering if you have any of that peach pie..."

I hardly heard the conversation about peach pie. Steve's mother had called his father Wild West. This time the words *wild* and *Wes* brought back a flash of memory. Something buried deep in the past. What was it? Something to do with friends. I remember thinking it was strange, because my mother didn't have many friends.

I was heading back to my truck, lost in thought, when the memory fell into place. I'd been sorting through my mother's papers after she died. I had to pay bills, find her bank account and the deed to the farm. My mother hadn't paid a bill in months. She'd just thrown everything into a drawer in her bedroom, where it had gotten mixed up with my little-kid drawings and the poems she'd written. In the jumble I'd found a scrap of paper folded into a tiny square. When I'd unfolded it, I saw a stranger's handwriting.

Wild Wes. With a phone number and area code I didn't recognize.

Ten

"**WHAT DID YOU** do with the paper?" Steve asked. That night over beers I'd filled him in on what I'd learned. He got more and more excited as I talked.

"Threw it out. Along with years of bills. I only kept her poems." I paused, wondering what I'd done with them. Poetry wasn't my thing, and hers didn't make much sense. Lots of dreams and death. But it was the closest thing I'd had to talking with her.

I dragged myself away from the sad

memory. "Does the name Wes ring a bell? Did your mother mention that name?"

Steve shrugged. "Sounds close to West. Sometimes she was hard to understand. She talked in whispers and ran out of breath easily. By the time she told me about my real father, she was near the end. When I asked her point-blank my father's last name, she just drifted off to sleep." He reached for another beer. Added the empty to the lineup. "It upset her, I think. And I wanted to make our last time together happy. Well, not happy but peaceful. I hid my own feelings the best I could. I just sat with her. Let her talk or not."

How different from my last few weeks with my own mother! After months of daydreaming on the sofa and sitting in the dark at night smoking, she was suddenly busy all the time. Shopping, gardening and working on her paintings in the back shed. She wouldn't let me see them. *I've got a commission*, was all she'd said. I thought she'd turned a corner.

After she died I found the paintings. Nothing but slashes of color—black, blood red, midnight blue, orange. The colors of a scream.

I grabbed some potatoes and began to scrub. Steve drank. "Anyway, it doesn't matter now," he said finally. "We have a name and a connection. Your uncle. We can talk to him tomorrow."

"No, we can't."

"Oh, he doesn't live around here anymore?"

"He does. But...we've lost touch." I chopped the potato fiercely. "The O'Tooles don't talk to me."

"What happened?"

"I happened."

Steve stared at me awhile, like the beer was slowing down his brain. "Jesus H.

Because your mother was unmarried? She was just a kid! And who does that these days?"

"The O'Tooles do. Back in the eighties in Lake Madrid, that was a mortal sin." I felt my face grow hot with the anger I'd held back. "They didn't care about God—they were mad at my mother for the shame. She was sixteen years old, in eleventh grade. And she wouldn't give me away. Wouldn't go stay with the nuns. She stayed right here in town and rubbed their noses in it."

"I get that they were mad. And ashamed. Small-town gossip can be nasty. But if we went to see them, I bet they'd be happy to see their own flesh and blood. All you have to do is break the ice."

"Don't hold your breath. You don't know them."

"Jesus H., Rick! Grow a pair! These people owe you!"

Rage flashed through me. I fought it back, hating the white-hot burn. "Don't you dare charge into my life and tell me how to live it! I've been doing just fine without you and any of the rest of the goddamn O'Tooles!"

"And I didn't come all this way just to have an old family grudge block me off."

"It's more than a family grudge! It's my... my..." I had no word for it.

We squared off across the table littered with beer bottles. Both of us breathing hard. "Do you want me gone?" Steve said finally.

"Maybe that's for the best."

"But do you *want* me gone?"

I hesitated. Confusion tangled my words. "I want my life back, before all of this. Before the dead guy and my uncle and all the memories."

"But do you want me *gone*?"

I couldn't answer him. I didn't know. I shoved the pot away and headed for the door. "The goat needs milking. You…you do whatever the hell you want."

A few minutes later, while I was out behind the barn, I heard the front door slam and his truck start up. I came around the barn just in time to see the plume of dust as he blasted out the gate.

Eleven

WHEN I WOKE up the next morning, Steve
was still gone. The place felt empty. Even
Chevy seemed lonely. Had Steve gone to
see my mother's family? Had he slept in his
truck?

I didn't have much time to wonder
before a police cruiser came down the road
and turned into my lane. Sergeant Hurley
climbed out. For once he wasn't smiling.
Beneath his steel-wool eyebrows, his eyes
bored into mine.

"I hear you been nosing around an old case."

I didn't know how much he knew, and I didn't want to get Jessica in trouble. So I said nothing.

"Where's this guy Steve?"

I shrugged. "Out on a bender or following up a lead."

"What lead?"

"He said he wanted to talk to my mother's family."

Hurley looked alarmed. "That's a real hornet's nest, Rick."

I got mad. I was tired of getting the runaround. "You investigated the accident. Why did you do such a crappy job?"

He blinked. I don't usually stand up to him. Or anyone else. "Who told you that?"

"People. You didn't interview witnesses, you didn't call in any crime-scene techs."

"Rick, this is none of your business."

"So people keep telling me! But it *is* my business. Steve says he's my half brother. And this dead man may be our father."

I could tell the news wasn't a surprise to him. He walked up to me and put his big hand on my shoulder. His eyes turned kind. I felt the anger drain out of me. Worse, tears started to form. "I've been waiting a long time to know," I managed.

He steered me toward the stoop. "There wasn't much to report," he said. "I did interview some witnesses who'd seen him at the Lion's Head. But they had nothing to add. I went out to the scene. I saw the curve, the drop and the tree halfway down. Once the tox results came in, it was pretty obvious what had happened. It happens all too often, Rick."

"What witnesses at the Lion's Head?"

"It's a long time ago. The regulars."

"My mother's brother, Tommy?"

Hurley looked down at his hands. "That's all I can say. There are privacy issues, Rick. I have to respect them."

"It's been almost thirty-five years! Whose privacy?"

He picked at a callused finger.

"I know the dead man's name was Wes. My mother knew him. Was he my father?"

Hurley squinted out across the field. Sighed. "Your mother...your mother didn't want your father's identity known. I know that seems unfair. But we should respect her wishes."

"My mother has been dead for seventeen years."

"She must have had her reasons."

"Do *you* know who my father was?"

"I do not."

I didn't believe him but knew I'd never get the secret out of him. His loyalty lay with my mother, even over me.

"Who would know?"

"Like you said, it's a long time ago."

"My grandparents? My uncle Tommy?"

"If they did, no one was talking to the cops."

His face had grown red. I wondered if there'd been an argument back then between the rookie-cop outsider and my mother's family. In February 1985 my mother would have been four months pregnant with me. Too pregnant to keep it a secret much longer. Her family would have been furious.

"It doesn't matter," I muttered. "If Steve went to talk to them, he won't take no for an answer."

"Holy hell," Hurley said. "That's not a good idea."

Then he got up and headed for his cruiser.

Twelve

ALL MORNING I worked on the deck at the Oland cottage. Usually I like this kind of work. It helps pay the bills, and I get to work by myself, out in the fresh air. But today I couldn't stop worrying about Steve. I wished we hadn't argued. I wished I'd told him to stay. I wished he hadn't gone off half-drunk to visit the O'Tooles. God only knew what he had said to them.

At noon I packed up my equipment and headed home, hoping to see his truck in the lane. No such luck. I checked my mother's bedroom and his gear was still there, clothes neatly folded and shoes lined up under the bed. You could bounce a dime off the bedspread. I drove into town to check the Lion's Head and Aunt Penny's. Steve was nowhere to be found.

I figured he hadn't given up and headed back to Calgary. He didn't own much stuff, but he couldn't afford to leave it behind. That left only one place to check.

My grandparents' house.

I knew where they lived, but I hadn't talked to them in several years. My grandfather had come to my mother's funeral, but he'd left without saying a word. For a few years after, I would drive over to their farm and park down the road. I'd watch my grandmother hanging out the wash, and my uncles drinking beer on the front porch. I tried to see myself in them, but they were all built like gorillas, squint-eyed and dirty.

The O'Toole place was over in the next township. It used to be a farm, but they'd let most of the land grow wild except for a couple of fields rented out to a farmer down the road. The house looked in better shape than I remembered it, and a fancy new sign was posted by the drive: *The Tool Guys*. My grandfather had started the business, but now Uncle Tommy ran it. I knew he was doing well because he got some of the big jobs in the county, and he drove a shiny new pickup with *The Tool Guys* on the side.

The truck wasn't out front when I arrived. Neither was Steve's truck. I tried to decide what to do. I wanted to leave. But I had to know if Steve had been here. After a few deep breaths to calm myself, I got out and started up to the house. The whine of a power saw stopped me. I headed instead to the workshop behind the house. Unlike my jumbled-up sheds, the place was big and bright. Stacks of lumber and half-finished cabinets lay on the floor. Tools and supplies filled the shelves. Three worktables sat in the middle.

An old man was standing at one of them, his legs planted wide apart for balance and his head bent over the two-by-six he was cutting. The saw was so loud he didn't hear me coming. I waited until he'd finished before speaking. He spun around, losing his balance and grabbing the table to stop his fall. He pushed his visor up and peered at me. His face was carved with wrinkles, and his eyes were sunk so deep they all but disappeared. Not a flicker of surprise or pleasure showed in them.

"I figured you'd come," he said. His voice was like chains being dragged over gravel.

My heart pounded. My damn tongue was in knots. "Hello," I said. Since I didn't know what to call him, I decided on nothing.

He grunted and walked past me. Scanned the yard before turning back to me. "What do you want?"

"You figured I'd come? So you've seen Steve?"

"Who's Steve?"

"Steve from Calgary. He says he's my half brother."

"You should know if he is or isn't," the old man said. "Far as I know, your mother only made that mistake once."

"I mean from my father."

We stared each other down. He swayed on his feet, so I reached out my hand. He jerked away and turned toward the porch. I joined him on the bottom step.

"What did you tell Steve?"

"I didn't see him."

"Then who did? My grandmother? Tommy?"

He shrugged. "You'll have to ask them."

"Granddad"—I forced myself to say the word—"I'm not a kid. I'm thirty-four years old. I can handle the truth. I want to know who my father is. I want to know if I have a brother."

My grandfather said nothing. An old mutt limped around the corner of the house, wagging its tail wearily. It flopped at his feet, and he leaned over to scratch its ears.

"Steve and I did some digging. There's a guy who died in a snowmobile accident just before I was born. He was visiting Tommy from Calgary. His name was Wes."

My grandfather bent his head and scratched harder. I thought his hand shook, but maybe he was just old.

"Why won't you tell me?" I said. "Mom and him are both dead. I don't have any family. You never wanted me. You cut my mother off like she was dirt."

"She did that to herself."

I could feel the heat building inside. Anger untied my tongue. "She was sixteen! She lost everything. It broke her heart!"

"And she broke her mother's heart."

Damn you. "I don't want anything from you. It's too late for that. But to know I have a brother..."

He was now shaking so hard that he clamped his hands between his knees. Finally he blew out a long breath. "I don't know, Cedric. Wes was a friend of Tommy's from the oil fields. He was a good-looking fella—all the girls in town were after him. This was when we lived out in your place. He stayed with us, and your mother...she took a shine to him. Begged him to take her on rides. Dirt bikes, snowmobiles, anything fast. Tommy laughed it off, said Wes was just like a big brother. But your grandmother was worried. She wanted Wes to leave. When your mother...well, when she came up in a family way, we told him to go. He said it wasn't his, but next we knew, he was gone."

"When was this?"

He didn't look at me. Pretended to be thinking. "Winter sometime? Same year you were born. We figured he'd run off back to Calgary."

"He was dead. You must have known that."

He shrugged. "Rumors. The cops never said a name."

"What was Wes's last name?"

"My memory's not what it used to be. But Tommy'll know. If he'll talk to you."

Something still didn't make sense. Why had my mother been blamed instead of the older man who had taken advantage? I asked Granddad that, and he turned red.

"Your grandmother's a good woman, but she's strict about the church and that. Your mother was turning out a bit of a wild one.

Makeup, music, dancing. Sneaking out at night. When your grandmother told her it was you or us, she chose you. Broke her mother's heart."

I hid my surprise at this new twist. I thought of all the times my mother had hugged me tightly, saying I was all she had. I backed up to safer ground. "Did you tell Steve any of this yesterday?"

"Like I said, I didn't see him."

"But he was here."

He shrugged. "I don't know. I was in town."

"Who was here then? My grandmother? Tommy?"

He didn't answer. Instead he turned to look at me. "Cedric, you're doing okay. I hear things. Folks talk. You've got the family touch." He held up his scarred old hands. "If this fella is your brother, I'm glad for you. The rest, the ancient history...let sleeping dogs lie."

It was almost like he was trying to be nice. It should have made me feel good. But behind the sad look on his wrinkled face, I thought I saw fear.

Thirteen

BACK AT MY farm there was still no sign of Steve. Chevy looked lonely as she ran down the lane to greet me. She jumped happily into the truck as we set off for another search. This time I drove all the backcountry roads and even along the highway to Hawley Bay. No maroon F-150. I dropped into the police station to see if there'd been any accidents.

Nothing.

As the afternoon wore on, I started to get mad. What was he playing at? The dude walks into my life, turns it upside down and then takes off because I didn't beg him to stay? Where the hell was he hiding out? Had he gone on a bender and decided to sleep it off in a roadside motel somewhere? Was he that close to the edge?

A sudden thought chilled me. I went into the barn where the shotgun was kept. Gone. I ran upstairs to check the ammunition box under my bed. Empty.

Shit.

Now I *had* to find Steve. Lake Madrid only had one pub, and I figured it was a good bet Steve had gone there sometime in the past day.

The pub was just getting ready for happy hour when I arrived. I sidled down to the dark corner of the bar where people might not notice me. When the bartender cocked one eyebrow at me, I ordered a half pint of beer. Big drinker, that's me.

When he brought it over, I lowered my voice. "I'm looking for a friend of mine, Steve, from Calgary. Cowboy hat, built like a fire hydrant. Has he been in?"

The bartender eyed me curiously. He is new to the village, but he likes to keep his ear to the ground. In his business, it pays to know your customers. "Yeah, he was in yesterday for a bit. Already tanked up and surly as a bear."

"Did he talk about anything? Like where he was going?"

"Not to me he didn't. He spilled his beer and that made him even madder. He turned around and yelled, *Is there anyone here who was in this shithole town back in 1985?*"

I sucked in my breath. "And what happened?"

"There was a table of punks over in that corner who volunteered. He snarled at them and yelled, *And old enough to remember?*"

"And?"

The bartender grinned and nodded to a man who had just walked in. "And Jack Ripley there said he was. They seemed to have a lot to say to each other, so maybe Jack knows where your friend is."

Jack Ripley owns a dairy farm outside town, and I've known him all my life. He hires me to help him with spring maintenance sometimes. We've never been real friends, but he's one of the good guys. He's as tough and strong as old leather, but his hair's white. I guess he's close to sixty. Old enough to remember 1985 perfectly.

Jack is a popular guy, and a few guys said hello as he was ordering his beer. Before he could join anyone else, I grabbed my beer and headed over.

"Jack, you got a minute?"

Jack's eyes flickered, but he didn't seem surprised. He nodded to a table in the corner.

"That way we can talk in private."

While I was still working out where to begin, he did it for me. "You're here about your brother?"

I blinked. "Steve told you that?"

He nodded. "He's mad that you won't go talk to the O'Tooles. I told him he didn't know the history. That it's a lot to ask of you."

I took a deep drink of my beer, collecting myself. "Did he ask you about the snowmobiler who died in 1985?"

He nodded. "Said it was his father. Your father."

"Do you remember him?" I asked. "Or the accident?"

He pursed his lips. "It was a long time ago."

More stalling. What the hell? "What *do* you remember? He was a friend of Tommy's. He stayed at my grandparents' house. What was he like?"

"Good-looking. Cocky. The life of the party, unless he'd had too much to drink."

"Did that happen often?"

Jack nodded. "We all partied too hard in those days. We were young men looking to create some excitement. Wes had a way about him of making you dream big, like the whole world could be yours. Most of the kids had never been out of the county and couldn't find Calgary on the map, but boy, they wanted to get on the next bus. But he was a flash in the pan, you know? He was here, he stirred things up, and then he was dead. Too much booze, too much speed, and it killed him." He stared into his glass. "It sure took the wind out of our sails."

I tried to picture the man who might be my father. He didn't seem like me. But it sounded like he could make my mother laugh. It made me sad. She had hardly ever laughed. Was she thinking of him all those times she sat dreaming in the dark?

"Do I remind you of him?" I asked.

Jack Ripley studied me for a long time. I figured he was trying to work out the best answer. "Now that I'm remembering, a bit. But you're more like your mother."

"Did he have blue eyes?"

"It was a long time ago. But yeah. He could be your dad."

I took a deep breath. Had I finally found my father? A stranger who'd blown into town like a whirlwind and swept a sixteen-year-old girl off her feet.

A stranger with a son of his own waiting for him in Calgary.

"What did you tell Steve?"

"More or less what I told you. But he wanted to know about the night he died. He wanted to know if I'd seen him."

"Had you?"

Jack took another long swig. His beer

was nearly empty. Normally, he only has one before he heads back to the farm. Cows don't give you much time off. But this time he waved to the bartender for a refill for both of us.

"Rick," he started, very slowly. "This is a lot for you. Learning who your father was. Finding out you might have a brother. These are big changes. I'm not sure it'll help. Do you really want to know about the night he died?"

It was like a cold draft raced through the room. Maybe a ghost. I shivered. I realized I was scared. Of the secret. Of whatever it was that no one wanted me to know. But Steve had not come home after he heard it. I needed to know why.

"I want to know what Steve learned."

He pursed his lips. Nodded. "Okay. A bunch of us were here at the Lion's Head. Wes, Tommy, Tommy's brother Kevin—he

moved up to the Yukon some years ago—
and maybe a couple of girls."

"My mother?"

He gave me a sharp look. "She was
sixteen, Rick. These were just some village
girls. Kevin took them home when Wes and
Tommy got into a fight."

"A fistfight?"

Jack shrugged. "Mostly yelling. Tommy
maybe threw one punch, but Wes didn't hit
back."

"What was the fight about?"

"It was just drunken bullshit."

"Jack!"

"Honest, Rick, it was bullshit."

"About my mother?"

"Look, I was trying not to listen. It was
over almost before it started, and then they
both took off. That was the days when you
could bring your sleds right up to the back
door, so off they went."

"Together? Tommy and Wes on one snowmobile?"

"Together, but Tommy had his own."

I sat back, stunned. Tommy had been with Wes on the night he died. The night he'd crashed his snowmobile and lain undiscovered for nearly a week. Dying a slow, freezing death. An accident, or something even worse? Had Tommy caused the crash? Was this the horrible secret everyone had been keeping from me all these years? Not to protect me, not to protect my mother, but to protect *Tommy*?

Jack was shifting in his chair, swirling his beer around and around. He cleared his throat a few times. "There's one other thing you should know, Rick. Only because Steve got it out of me, and better you hear it from me than from him. Tommy had his own sled, but your mother...she was waiting out back for Wes. Maybe that was what the argument was about. And she got on the back with Wes."

I felt like the floor had opened up. I was falling through. Had my mother known too? Had she been involved? And left the father of her unborn child—*my father*—to die alone in the snow?

I heard my voice from very far away. "Did you tell the police any of this?"

"Yeah. Rob Hurley."

Fourteen

MY HEAD WAS spinning when I left the bar. I tried to make sense of what Jack had said. Hurley had known from the beginning about Tommy, my mother and the fight that night. But he'd put none of it in his report. He had to figure one or both of them had been involved in the accident and had done nothing to help. Instead they'd left my father to die. Why?

I didn't want to think about why. Even if it explained all the crazy secrets of the last thirty-four years. My mother hadn't been the best mother in the world, but she'd tried. And she'd called children's services when she couldn't. I still had memories of her rocking me in her arms. Humming a tune or whispering funny stories in my ear. I remembered her sticking labels all around the house and playing word games to try to teach me to read.

But she'd been lost in another world a lot of the time. Was this why? Was she stuck back in that night, reliving the crash, the panic and the decision to leave Wes in the snow? Had he been conscious? Had he screamed for help? Was this the picture she could never erase from her mind? The way I could never erase the afternoon when Hurley took me to see the rock face?

In the back of my mind was another question I'd never wanted to face. Had my mother hit that rock face on purpose? Aunt Penny had once said none of it was my fault.

That my mother had depressions, just like her mother before her. But maybe the rock face was her way of escaping forever the ghosts that hounded her. Had this been the ghost she couldn't escape?

After a while I began to get beyond that awful thought. Maybe she hadn't walked away from the crash on her own. Maybe it was Tommy who'd dragged her away. She was sixteen, and he was ten years older, a big man in his prime. Or maybe she'd been hurt, even unconscious, and Tommy had picked her up, put her on his snowmobile and taken her home. Maybe she didn't remember the accident and didn't know Wes was dead until the body was found. And by then maybe Tommy had sworn her to secrecy, saying they would both be charged.

It was a small light of hope, but I wanted to hang on to it. Was it enough to explain her guilt and the rock face?

There was only one person who knew. Now, finally, I was going to have to face him, because I knew Steve wouldn't have hesitated. Like an army tank, he would have gone straight over to confront him.

With a loaded shotgun in his truck.

Folks in town say Uncle Tommy is a straight-up kind of guy who never cheats his customers or cuts corners on a job. But back in the days when he was drinking, he had a bad temper. I didn't know how he'd react to Steve or to me. I didn't want a fist to the head. I knew he was working on a cottage by the lake, on the other side of town. I hoped he'd be civil to me with the cottage owner in earshot.

But there was only one vehicle in the cottage's gravel lane. A new black pickup with *The Tool Guys* on the side. My heart beat faster, and my palms turned sweaty. I parked beside it, and as soon as I climbed out, I heard the hammer. I found him on the other side of the wood frame, hammering a plywood subfloor. I hadn't seen him in at least ten years. He had a shaved head and a full beard that was mostly gray. Tattoos crawled over his leathery skin. At the sound of my footsteps, he looked up.

He said nothing.

"You know why I'm here?" I asked.

He looked down and slammed in a nail. One blow, dead accurate.

"Did Steve come to see you?"

Another nail down.

"He's missing. Do you know anything about that?"

He was lining up for a third nail.

"Damn it, Uncle Tommy! Look at me, you bastard!"

It was the wrong word to use. He stopped, his hammer in the air, and looked up. "Look who's calling me that."

I walked over to sit on a stool and tried to

stop shaking. "I don't care what you think of me, and I don't care if you never talk to me again. But like it or not, I am your nephew. All my life I've had no one but my mother. You guys washed your hands of us. It was a cruel thing to do to an innocent kid. Okay fine, I can live with that. But it would be nice to have a brother. I know Steve came to see you. What did you tell him?"

"Never saw him."

I tried again for calm. "He may have been drunk. He may have been in rough shape, even—" I stopped short of saying *violent*. "He's been through a lot, three tours in Afghanistan, shot up his leg, just lost his mother. So now he wants to know...we think our father was this guy Wes who came to stay with you, the guy who died in a snowmobile accident."

The hammer came down. Crooked. "Who's been telling you this shit?"

"Jack Ripley. He was at the bar with you that night, remember? He says you and Wes left together and my mother was on the back of Wes's snowmobile."

"Jack Ripley was drunk as a skunk. He wouldn't have noticed if Jesus himself had come into the bar."

"He made a lot of sense just now." I pressed my hands together to hide their shaking. I couldn't do anything about my voice. "What the hell happened that night, Tommy? Did you—"

"Leave it, Rick!" Tommy's voice cracked like a whip. "No good will come from digging it all up."

I felt tears gathering. *Jesus, not now.* "No good for me, or for you?"

"For anyone. I don't know what happened. We went our separate ways. What the hell do you think?"

"Is that what you told Steve?"

"Like I said, never saw him."

"I know him. He'd go straight from Jack Ripley to you, looking for answers." And now he's disappeared, I thought with a jolt of fear. "What the hell happened?"

"Don't know what you're talking about," Tommy said. He stood up stiffly and walked over to pack up his toolbox. "I don't know where he is, but from the sound of it, you're better off without him."

Fifteen

THE SUN WAS low on the horizon when I got back to the farmhouse. By then I no longer expected to find Steve. I didn't know if he was holed up somewhere, brooding, off on a new search or living out some nightmare in his head. I went into the kitchen to get Chevy's food and spotted the blinking light on the battered old answering machine that sat in the corner. I'd rescued it from the dump, given it a little tweaking, and it was all I needed. I hardly ever got messages, but now my pulse leaped. Why hadn't I checked it earlier?

When I pressed the Replay button, I heard only silence at first. Then breathing. Then: "Rick? Rick?" and some whispers. One word sounded like "help."

I turned up the volume and replayed it. "Help." Very weak and shaky, not like Steve's booming voice at all.

I replayed it still louder. Between all the hisses and crackles of the old machine, I heard the words "help" and "tool."

Tool? I stared at the machine. Maybe he'd said O'Toole. I could make no more sense of the message, with all the hisses and crackles, but my heart pounded. Steve was in trouble. He'd asked for help. How long ago? Today? Yesterday?

I had only one clue, but it would have to do. After tossing some food into Chevy's bowl, I grabbed my keys and headed out.

For the second day in a row, I drove the backcountry road toward my grandparents' place. This time I was not going to take *I don't know* for an answer!

There's not much to see along that road. Mostly empty scrub that used to be pastures, now taken over by poplar and cedar. A couple of boarded-up houses no one has lived in for years. The original farmers are dead, their kids all moved to the city. Faded For Sale signs hang crooked out front, but no one's buying. I didn't see a single vehicle as I drove along. The setting sun glared across the fields, and the shadows were sharp. Something deep in the gully caught the light. A tricky turn was coming up, but I slowed enough to take a quick look down the steep drop. A stream ran through the thick brush, and in the midde of the brush, wedged upside down against a tall willow, was a truck.

I slammed on my brakes. Within seconds I was racing down the hill, following the deep ruts made by tires in the tall grass. Up close, I saw the truck was a maroon F-150. Steve's truck! Its wheels were in the air, and its cab was crushed. I prayed he'd jumped out before and was walking home across the fields, because it didn't look like there could be anyone alive inside. But when I rounded the truck, I saw him. He'd crawled halfway out the broken window and lay bleeding all over a patch of lilies.

His eyes were shut, and he was as white as a ghost. I screamed at him. Not even a twitch. My hands shook so hard I could hardly feel his pulse. He was *alive!*

I grabbed a blanket from his truck and covered him. I had to call 9-1-1, and fast. But I wasn't one for high-tech stuff, so I had no cell phone. I couldn't see his. Cursing, I scrambled back up the hill. I tried to remember where the nearest house was. My grandfather's. I jumped in my truck and took off in a storm of gravel. At the farmhouse, a 1996 Corolla covered in mud and rust sat in the yard. Before I even got to the front door, an old woman appeared at the screen door and blocked my way. She had only a couple of teeth left, in a face like one of last year's potatoes.

"Be on your way," she said. "We got nothing to say to you."

"Steve's been in an accident! I need to call 9-1-1!"

She nodded up the road. "MacLeod's place is just over the hill."

All those years of hurt and anger rushed in. I wanted to strangle her. "There's no time! He's hurt bad!"

"We don't want trouble."

It was a weird thing to say, but I was in no mood to argue. "Grandma—"

"Don't you call me that!"

Sharp tears stung my eyes. I was about to shove her when a shadow appeared behind her. "Let him call, Maeve," my grandfather said. "You go out and tend to the hens. I'll show him the phone."

My grandmother didn't move until my grandfather reached around her to let me in. She shrank back like I had a disease and turned her back. "Then you be gone!" she snapped as she stomped down the hall.

I calmed down a bit when I'd got through to 9-1-1 and explained where Steve was. The lady assured me the ambulance was on its way. When I hung up, my grandfather was at my side with a pile of blankets and towels in his arms.

"I'd go with you, son, but..." He glanced through the kitchen window, where my grandmother could be seen taking a pitchfork to the muck in the chicken coop. It wouldn't do to cross her.

I took the blankets. "Thanks, Granddad."

He shuffled after me to the door. "I hope he's all right."

I thanked him again and took off.

As I approached the scene, I saw a truck parked on the side of the road. Darkness was falling, but I could make out *The Tool Guys* on the side. When I peered down into the gully, I saw Tommy moving behind the crushed truck. I couldn't see Steve, but it looked like Tommy was bent over him, beating him.

I raced down the hill, shouting. Tommy looked up and stepped back. When I rounded the truck, Steve was splayed on his back in the grass. Blood trickled from his mouth. Tommy's hands were covered with blood.

"What are you doing!" I screamed.

Tommy gestured at Steve. "He's hurt bad. I saw his truck on my way home, came down—"

"You were killing him!"

"I was doing CPR!" Tommy retorted. "He stopped breathing and—"

"Bullshit!" I was so frightened and angry I could hardly think. "I saw you hitting him."

"Yeah! CPR! And if we don't continue—"

"Not like this, it isn't." I waved my fist to show him what I'd seen.

Tommy's face turned dark. He started toward me. I backed up. "The cops and paramedics are on their way," I said.

"What do you think, Cedric? That I'm a murderer?"

I strained my ears for the sound of a siren. I wanted to find out the truth, but I was no match for Tommy. "I don't know. I just know what I saw."

"Which you can tell the cops or not."

I glanced behind him at Steve. I couldn't tell if he was breathing. Had Tommy already killed him? Rage crashed through me. "And you killed our father too, didn't you? That's what Steve figured out. Why did you do it? Because he got my mother pregnant?

Or was it just a stupid, drunken fight?"

"It was an accident."

"If it was, why did you leave him there? Why did you let him die?"

Tommy came closer. His face was like a thundercloud. "I told you, let it go, Cedric."

"Not after this!" I waved at Steve. "After thirty-four years of hell, you dare to take him away from me too?"

He gripped my shoulder in a vise and clenched his fist. I was taller than him, but he had a good fifty pounds on me. I stared at his fist, gnarled and scarred. "Go ahead! Hit me!"

His eyes flickered. He loosened his grip and shoved me back. Finally, in the distance, a siren wailed.

"I'm not what you think, Cedric," he said, and he turned to walk up the hill.

Sixteen

I WATCHED THE clock on the hospital wall. Time ticked by, hour after hour. They'd put me in a quiet little waiting room near the intensive care unit. Steve was in surgery. I figured as long as he was in surgery, he was still alive. I held on to that.

I replayed those last minutes when the paramedics were loading him into the ambulance. He hadn't moved when I put my hand on his shoulder and leaned over him. "Steve. Hang in there, buddy. I'll be right behind you."

Nothing. Not a moan or a blink of his eyes. He breathed slowly and weakly, like he was slipping away.

Jessica had arrived on the scene with her partner at the same time as the ambulance. She'd studied me with her gentle blue eyes. Jessica was getting good at reading my mind.

"You go to the hospital. I'll catch you there after I've examined the scene."

The hospital was twenty-five miles away. I'd pushed my old pickup down the highway as fast as I dared. By the time I reached the hospital, Steve was being prepared for surgery.

"Who's his next of kin?" a clerk asked.

Without thinking, I'd said, "Me." Then blood had rushed to my head, and I'd had to lean on the counter.

The clerk had given me a suspicious look. She was from back home, and she knew I had no next of kin—or, at least, kin that would speak to me. But she gave me some papers to sign and told me to sit in the waiting room. Someone would come out to talk to me. Eventually.

Pacing the waiting room, I thought about everything Steve had gone through. The wars in Afghanistan, the death of his mother, the news of his father. I thought about how he'd cleaned up my sheds and made eggs in the morning and scratched Chevy's ears. I thought about coming downstairs in the morning to the smell of fresh coffee, served with a big, hopeful grin.

And I realized what we meant to each other. Family. History. A place in this world.

Don't die on me, brother! I begged as the clock ticked on.

When the doctors wheeled Steve out, they weren't making any promises. They talked about putting more pins in his leg, taking out parts of his insides, opening up his skull. They were patient and under-standing with me, but I could hardly make sense of the words. I just nodded and wished Jessica was with me.

She came just as dawn was peeking over the rooftops. She was still in her uniform, and she looked worn out, but she managed a hug for me.

"Sergeant Hurley will be along later this morning to take a statement from you," she said. "He's called in a full investigation team."

"Because of Tommy?"

She hesitated. Pulled at her fingers. "What was Steve's mood when you last saw him?"

I felt sick. We'd argued, and he'd driven off in a state. Drunk and looking for a fight. "Not good," I mumbled. "What? You think he drove off the road on purpose?"

"There were some bits of broken glass and debris on the road. His truck has a broken right taillight. Was it like that before?"

"Steve loved that truck. He'd have fixed it right away. It was probably broken in the crash."

She was silent. My heart pounded. "What are you saying?"

"There was another set of tire marks on the shoulder too."

A chill shot through me. "Someone *drove* him off the road?"

"That's for the investigation team to decide. It's a narrow road, and it gets dark as pitch at night. The evidence suggests he was there since yesterday." She looked at me. "What was Steve doing on that road, Rick?"

I tensed. Her voice was gentle, but it sounded like an interrogation. "He was going to visit my grandparents."

She didn't look surprised. Like she'd

already guessed. "Then he'd already been there. He was driving away."

My brain finally started putting pieces together. He'd visited my grandparents, probably had a fight with Tommy and driven off in a rage. With Tommy hot on his heels.

I started to shake. Jessica put her arm around me. "Have you eaten anything?"

When I shook my head, she stood up. "I have to call Hurley, and I could use a coffee. I'll get us both something from the cafeteria."

I knew I couldn't eat, but I didn't argue. I wanted time to get myself together.

After she left I heard heavy footsteps coming down the hall. A second later Tommy appeared in the doorway. I rose from my seat.

"What the hell are you doing here?"

"How is he?"

"Alive. No thanks to you."

He looked relieved. "I told you, I was

doing CPR. I probably saved his miserable life, you jerk."

"Yeah? What about when you ran him off the road? You left him to die, just like you did—"

"I did no such thing!"

"They found tire tracks! They'll examine your truck!"

His eyes grew wide. He looked cornered.

"He came to the house, didn't he? He asked you about Wes's death. Probably said you killed him. You've been keeping this crazy secret for more than thirty-four years, and you weren't about to pay for it now. So you chased him down and drove him off the road."

Tommy paced the little room. "It didn't happen that way. It was an accident."

"You smashed into his truck!"

"He cut me off and slammed on his brakes. I couldn't stop."

"Why would he do that?"

"He was psycho. He fired at me out his window! I was just trying to outrun him." He paused. "Man, that guy can drive!"

My brain spun. Refused to take it in. "Then why didn't you call the cops? Why did you just leave him there? A whole day he lay down there, bleeding out."

"I didn't know he'd flipped his truck! It was dark, and he had a gun!" Tommy took a deep breath to calm down. "I knew if I called the cops, it would bring up all the old crap about Wes's death again. I decided I'd just get the hell out, and if the cops came, they'd put it down to an accident. He was drunk, and lots of people lose control on that curve."

I stared at him. Was that possible? It was the longest speech he'd ever made to me. He had to be really scared. "Then why did you come back?"

"Because you told me he was missing. I thought I should check on him."

"To make sure he was dead."

He grew red. "No. To see if he was there. If he needed help."

I wasn't sure I believed him, but I was too tired to think. Besides, I had other questions. "What was the old crap about Wes's death?"

"Jesus, let's not dig up all this again. You know!"

"No, I don't know! I know you were with him. I know you and my mother left him to die alone and never said a word. I know that for a whole week the coyotes and crows had a field day."

"It's not quite true we never said a word. Your mother told Hurley."

It was my turn to be shocked. I stared at him. "What are you talking about?"

"Hurley knew. At least, your mother said she told him. He had a thing for her, and she figured he'd go easy on her."

"She was sixteen!"

"Hurley wasn't much older. Only on the job a few months."

I shut my eyes. I wished I could shut off my brain too. But thirty-four years was too long. "What happened that night, Uncle Tommy?"

He stood up to go. "I told you to leave it be. Wes and your mother are both dead."

"Then it won't matter to them. But it matters to me. Did you ram him? Was it deliberate?"

He froze. "What the hell? No! We were joyriding. Going way too fast. He lost control."

"Was my mother on the snowmobile with him?"

He looked away.

"Was she hurt?" I grasped at straws. "Knocked out?"

"No, she jumped off."

I thought about that. "She jumped off and let him go over the ravine."

"She was lucky, Rick. She wasn't drunk like he was."

"Whose idea was it to just leave him there?"

"Well, we had to, right? There were no cell phones in those days. We went into town to call the cops."

"Did you check on him? See if he was alive?"

He hesitated. "Yeah, he was alive. But your mother...she wanted to get the hell out. She knew she'd be in big trouble if our mother found out."

"She was pregnant with his child! Didn't that count for something?"

He shot me a glance. "She was sixteen, Rick."

"So she called Hurley."

"And nothing happened." He bowed his head in defeat. "So after a week I rode back up there and pretended to find him."

I heard light footsteps in the hall. Jessica was on her way back. What the hell was I going to tell her? My mother was dead, but her boss, months from retirement, was still very much alive. Did he have blood on his hands?

seventeen

THE SECRET TORMENTED me. I kept it to myself
for three days, sitting by Steve's bedside,
tending to my farm and sharing quiet walks
with Jessica. I didn't tell her what Tommy
had told me about Steve's accident. I was
waiting to see what the cops came up with
on their own. The doctors said Steve's heart
had stopped a couple of times in the ambulance and on the operating table. He had
bruises and a broken rib probably caused
by CPR.

Maybe Tommy wasn't such a monster after all. If he was telling the truth about Steve, was he also telling the truth about the night my father died? Had they left him to die because my mother was afraid of getting into trouble? Had Tommy really left it up to her to call Hurley? He was twenty-six, she sixteen. When Hurley did nothing, why hadn't Tommy checked with him?

What if my mother hadn't phoned Hurley at all? What if she'd deliberately let my father die and taken that awful guilt to her grave?

So many questions. Only one person knew the answers. Hurley.

I knew he'd never admit to it. Not with his career and years of service on the line.

Three days later the answers began to come, from a source I'd forgotten all about. I came home from visiting Steve late one afternoon and found a car parked in my lane. It was Dan Picard.

"Jeez, Rick," he exclaimed as he climbed out, "don't you ever check your messages?"

I got him one of Steve's beers, and we sat together on the front stoop. He held out an old, yellowed newspaper. "I found the article you wanted. If you can call it an article. Nothing but a two-inch snippet on an inside page." He started to read. "*An Alberta man, visiting the area to go snowmobiling and ice fishing, died last week in a late-night snowmobile mishap north of town. There was no moon, and alcohol is believed to be a factor. The curve where the man lost control is well known among local daredevils. Police are investigating, and the victim's identity is being withheld pending notification of next of kin.*"

He put the paper aside. "I searched later issues for more news, like the results of the police investigation or an update on the man's identity. Nothing. When you think a stray dog gets better coverage in the local rag, it got me curious. So I went to see Simon Larose."

"Who's Simon Larose?"

"He ran the paper from 1972 to 1998. He's living with his daughter in the city now, but he's sharp as a tack and bored silly. I showed him the paper and asked him if he could remember anything else. As clear as if it was yesterday, he said. The man's name was Wesley Campbell from Calgary. According to the police, the O'Toole family, who he was visiting, said he had no next of kin. So in the end, someone paid for him to be buried in the Presbyterian Church grave-yard up at Watkins Corners. There was no funeral, and as far as I know, the grave is unmarked."

"But he did have a family," I said. "He had a girlfriend and a son out west. No one ever told them he'd died. They thought he'd just run off."

Dan shrugged. "Well, either Tommy didn't know that, or he lied."

"Did Tommy pay for the burial?"

"No. That's the odd thing. Simon said it was the cop who was on the case at the time. Rob Hurley."

The next morning I stood outside the door of the police detachment, gathering my nerve. I had a lot of questions for Sergeant Hurley. But I always felt like that four-year-old kid in the back of the cop car whenever I saw him. The glass front door had an invitation to his retirement party taped to it.

I pushed through the door and made my way to his office at the back. I had my anger all ready, but he smiled and asked me how Steve was doing. I felt my anger fizzle.

"Recovering," I said, trying to get it back, "but we have questions for you."

He tipped his chair back. "Shoot."

"About our father's death. You were the one who investigated the accident."

His chair thudded forward. "Like I told you, straightforward case."

"Why didn't you interview witnesses? Or order forensics?"

"It was a dark, dangerous curve, and he was drunk. You don't order forensics for every little case."

"Why did you keep his identity secret? Why didn't you notify his family back in Calgary?"

"I didn't know about them."

"But why didn't you check?"

He gave me a long, hard look. "Tommy O'Toole said he had none."

I tried to hide my shaking. None of this made any sense. "I know Tommy and Wes had a fight that night. I know my mother drove off with him. But nobody found him for a week! That's pretty fishy!"

Hurley stood up and came around his desk. He was so close I could smell his stale sweat. "The man was dead, Ricky. Bringing their names into it wouldn't have helped anyone. Your mom was sixteen. She'd lost the man she loved, and she was pregnant. She'd had enough hurt."

I thought of all the times Hurley had protected my mother. Maybe it had all started with this. "Why did you pay for his burial?"

Hurley blinked in surprise. For a minute I thought he was going to deny it, but then he sighed. "I did it for your mother. To give her some peace of mind. She couldn't afford to pay, and she sure couldn't ask her parents." He looked at me sadly. "I'm sorry you never knew about your father all these years, Ricky. When your mother died, I thought about telling you, but I figured it would just add salt to your wounds."

He made it all sound so reasonable. But I knew he'd had thirty-four years to figure out a cover-up, and my mother wasn't around to say different. I had one last question that still needed an answer.

"Tommy says on the night my father died, my mother told him she'd call you. Did she?"

Hurley looked at the ceiling. He was caught in the middle, and he knew it. My father had been left to the coyotes for almost a week. Either Hurley knew, or he didn't.

"Yeah," he said finally. "But not till a day later. I did a drive-by, but he was frozen stiff. So…I left him, to keep your mother out of it. In my thirty-five years, it's one thing that sticks with me. But Tommy should never have left it up to her."

Eighteen

WE DIDN'T TALK much on the drive through the countryside. Steve leaned against the headrest and shut his eyes. The past week had been exhausting. The cops had hounded him about the accident. He said he remembered only bits. He remembered shouting at Tommy. Tommy taking off. He remembered chasing Tommy's truck through the dark. Spoiling to fight.

I wasn't sure I should push him, but I needed to know one more thing. "Steve, the cops found my shotgun near your truck. It had been fired. Do you remember shooting it?"

He opened his eyes and looked at me. I saw fear in his eyes. He shook his head.

"It could have gone off in the crash," I said.

Still Steve said nothing, but his chin trembled.

"I never liked it anyway." I said. "Maybe I'll get rid of it."

Finally the ghost of a smile crossed his face. "Good idea."

I felt a wave of relief. It wasn't much, but for a guy who'd wanted that gun by his side, it was a start. Maybe he was going to be okay.

Up ahead, a little church sat at the empty crossroads that had once been Watkins Corners. It was built of limestone the locals had probably dug up with their own hands over a hundred years back. It had a steeple, a rusty bell and a peeling sign outside that gave the times of the services.

The graveyard too had seen better times. A couple of headstones had bits of dried flowers on them. Someone had mowed the grass near the church, but the rest was overrun with weeds. Steve had phoned the church from his hospital room. He'd spoken to the sexton, who had given him the general location of our father's grave.

Steve studied the paper in his hand and pointed. "It should be in the northeast corner, near the far fence."

There was nothing but overgrown grass and weeds in that corner. Steve was leaning on his cane, already worn out. I wanted to tell him to wait while I searched. But I knew he'd never agree. So we set out, kicking a path through the tall grass. As we neared the far fence, I swept the weeds away with my foot.

"I guess he's around here somewhere," I muttered.

Steve poked. His cane hit something hard. He parted the grass and uncovered the edge of a plaque. "Look!"

"But Dan Picard said the grave was unmarked," I said.

Steve ignored me. He pushed more weeds aside. "Rick? Doesn't that say…"

I peered. There it was—a small brass plaque gone green with age. Together we stared at it. There wasn't much on it, and the letters were worn. *Wesley Campbell. Born June 5, 1957. Died February 20, 1985. Rest in Peace.*

I didn't know what to say. I didn't know what to feel. It was just a plaque in the ground. Marking the death of a stranger. This was the end of my search. I thought I should feel more.

Steve heaved a deep sigh, like his search was over too.

"Do you remember him at all?" I said.

He shook his head. "I was only four when he left."

I looked around. It was a peaceful place. An old oak gave some shade. The breeze was soft, and bees buzzed in the clover beside the fence. Cows dotted the pasture in the distance.

I felt something give inside me. A coiled spring I hadn't even known was there. I leaned over to rub the stains on the plaque. "With some vinegar and salt, this will look new again."

"Or we could get him a proper headstone."

"That would cost money."

"I've got money."

"But..." How could I explain it? His father was dead because of my family. My mother had only been sixteen, but she and Tommy were the ones who had left him. She was the one who didn't call for help.

Steve grinned. Punched me in the arm, almost like the old Steve. "And you've got all that stuff I can sell on Kijiji."

"Okay. I'd like that." So would my mother. A small start at putting things right.

"And after this," he said, "we'll go check if our DNA kits have arrived."

"Yeah, okay," I said. "But I don't think we need them."

We stood side by side, looking at the plaque. Finally Steve spoke. "About that DNA. Maybe we shouldn't bother?"

A smile spread through me. "No. We're good."

ACKNOWLEDGMENTS

In the beginning, writers work alone to create their stories, but many other people help to make those stories even better. First I'd like to thank my good friend and fellow writer Vicki Delany, who read *Blood Ties* and made helpful suggestions. I also want to thank all the staff at Orca Book Publishers for their enthusiastic help and their support both of me and of Rapid Reads short novels in general. Most of all, a huge thank-you to Orca's associate publisher, Ruth Linka, for making *Blood Ties* the best book it can be.

BARBARA FRADKIN is a child psychologist with a fascination for how people turn bad. Her compelling short stories haunt numerous magazines and anthologies, but she is best known for her two series of gritty, psychological novels, one featuring Ottawa police inspector Michael Green and the more recent one with foreign-aid worker Amanda Doucette. Barbara won Arthur Ellis Best Novel Awards for both *Fifth Son* (2005) and *Honour Among Men* (2007). Her work as a school psychologist helping adolescents and younger children, many of whom struggle with reading, has also made her a strong advocate of programs that help develop reading as a lifelong passion. She lives in Ottawa.